D1541255

Printed in the United States
ISBN: 978-0-9819861-4-2

Written by Eli Kowalski
Illustrated by Jim McWeeney
Cover and Interior Design by Ilene Griff Design

Philadelphia, PA 19102
267-847-9018
www.sportschallengenetwork.com

Kushka

the Dog Named Cat

by
Eli Kowalski

illustrated by
Jim McWeeney

HUGS AND KISSES

KUSHKA

We have a dog, whose name means cat.

Have you ever heard anything as silly as that?

We call her our
Kushka,
that's Russian,
you see . . .

Kushka means kitty, between you and me.

She looks like a dog but acts like a cat.

Have you ever seen a dog behave quite like that?

Kushka is **fluffy,** with silky white hair.

She likes to eat popcorn and JUMP in the air.

She likes to wear hats on her little white hea

nd has every color from **purple** to red.

Kushka is busy most of her day.

She's not sure if she wants to sleep or to Play!

She plays and she sleeps,
she sleeps and she plays.

Wouldn't you
like to do that all
of your days?

Her best friend is Bernie,
a stuffed Saint Bernard.

She sleeps on his back, which is soft and not hard.

And Sammy, her teddy bear
snuggles real close,

with pretty brown
eyes and a cute
button nose.

They both come
to life when there's
no one around.

But when people are watching
they don't make a sound.

The three of them play and have fun all day long.

And sometimes
they act out this
cute little song:

RADIO

Red light, green light, run around the house,

Spin left, spin right, quiet as a mouse.

Then Kushka, Bernie and Sammy,
all three, lie down on the
floor to watch TV.

After watching awhile, they then play with toys.

They **run** and they *jump* but without too much noise.

After a day of having so much fun, Kushka likes to take a nap in the warm sun.

She dreams about all her toys throughout the house.

Which one is next that she is going to pounce?

She wakes up an.

All of a sudden, Kushka
hears a **loud sound.**
She turns her head and looks all around.

To get a better look,

just like a cat, she leaps up in the a i r,

and lands
softly on top of
her daddy's chair.

Just in the nick of time, her mommy arrives.

And Kushka jumps UP to give her **high fives!**

Kushka wonders if he brought her something new to explore.

Daddy is next through the door.

Daddy and Kushka will
play a doggy game,
until it's time to eat dinner,
then more of the same.

When it's time to go out,
her little tail wags.

We carry her out in
one of her bags.

We get to the street and she **jumps** out to explore,

and smiles to our neighbors as we pass each door.

When Kushka comes back home, she gets a treat.

She knows that her day is almost complete!

Now that she's tired
and after she's fed,

Kushka is ready to climb into our bed.

She kisses her mommy and daddy good-night,

and falls
asleep knowing
that everything
is just right.

Kushka's long
day has now come
to an end.

She will wake us up tomorrow with
kisses and do it again.